For my mother

First published in the United States and Canada in 2014 by Lemniscaat USA LLC • New York
Distributed in the United States by Lemniscaat USA LLC • New York

Cataloging-in-publication data is available.
van Hout, Mies
Surprise! / Written and illustrated by Mies van Hout
1. Emotions - Juvenile Fiction. 2. Parenting-Juvenile Fiction. 3. Birds-Juvenile Fiction.
PZ7 [E]

ISBN 978-1-935954-34-7 (Hardcover)
Printed in the United States by Worzalla, Stevens Point, Wisconsin
First U.S. Edition
www.lemniscaatusa.com

MIES VAN HOUT

Surprise

LEMNISCAAT

Yearning

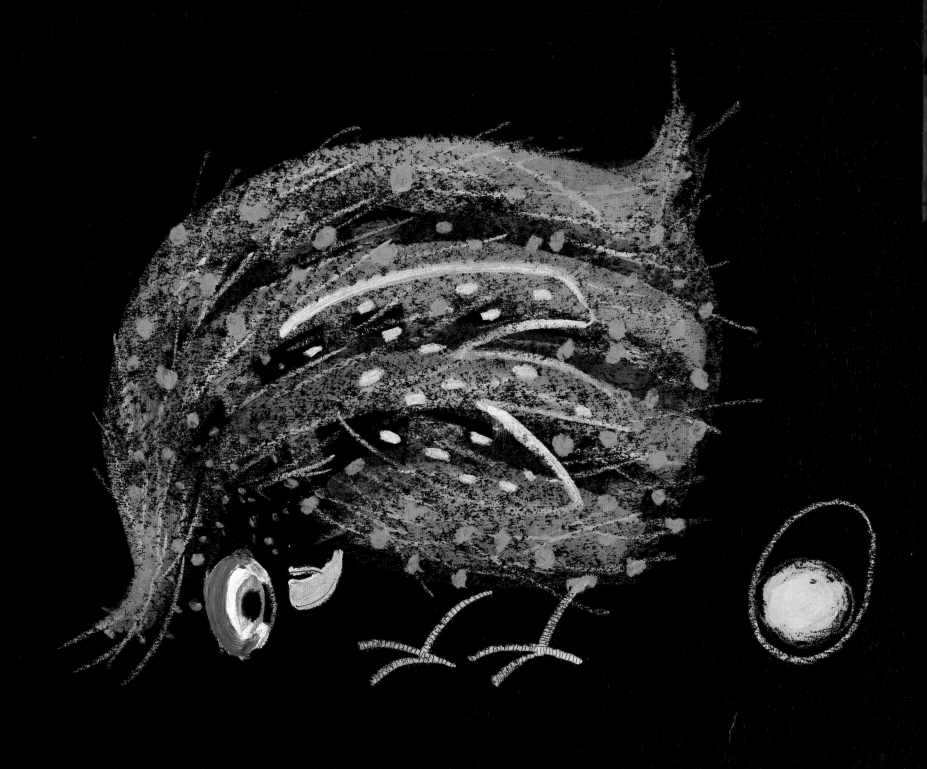

expecting

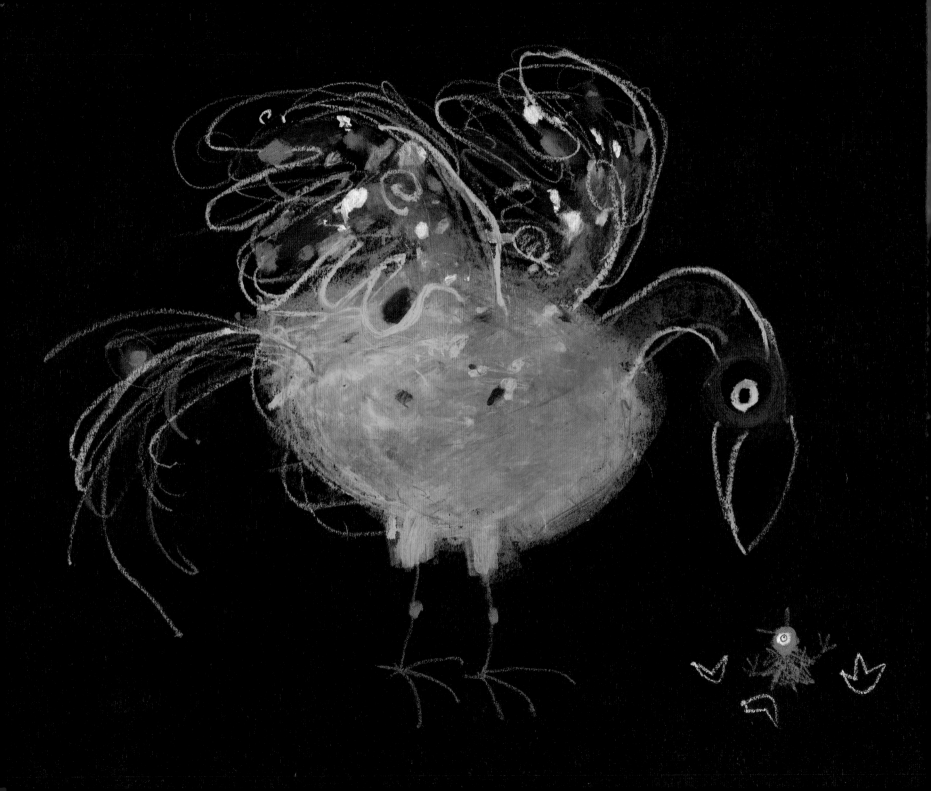

marveling

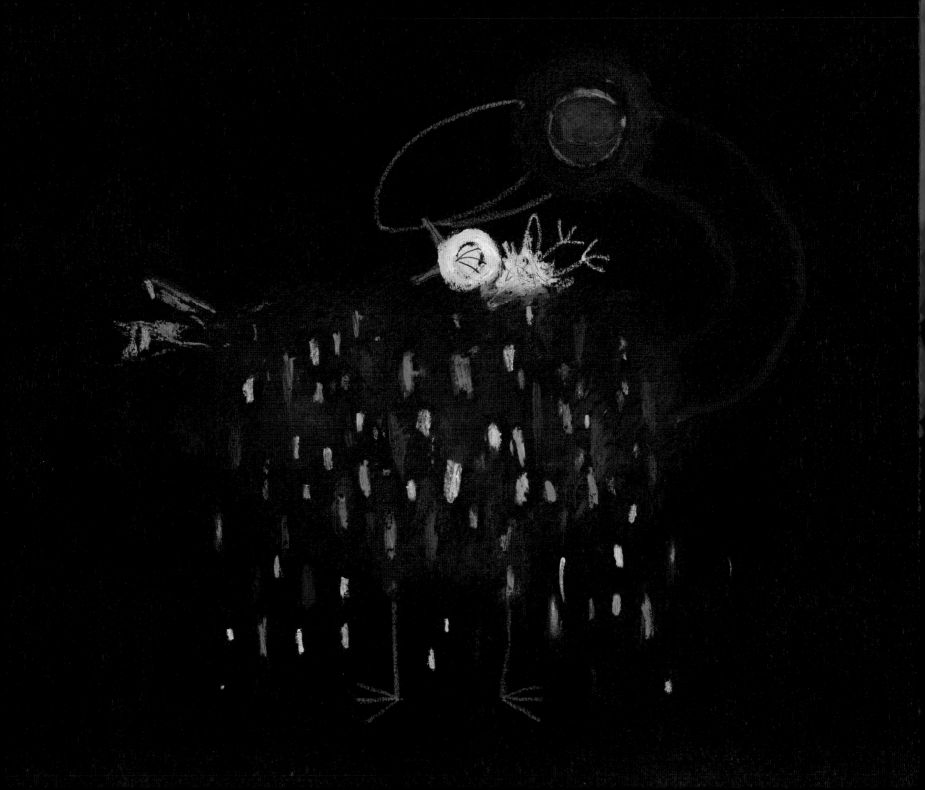

comforting

cherishing

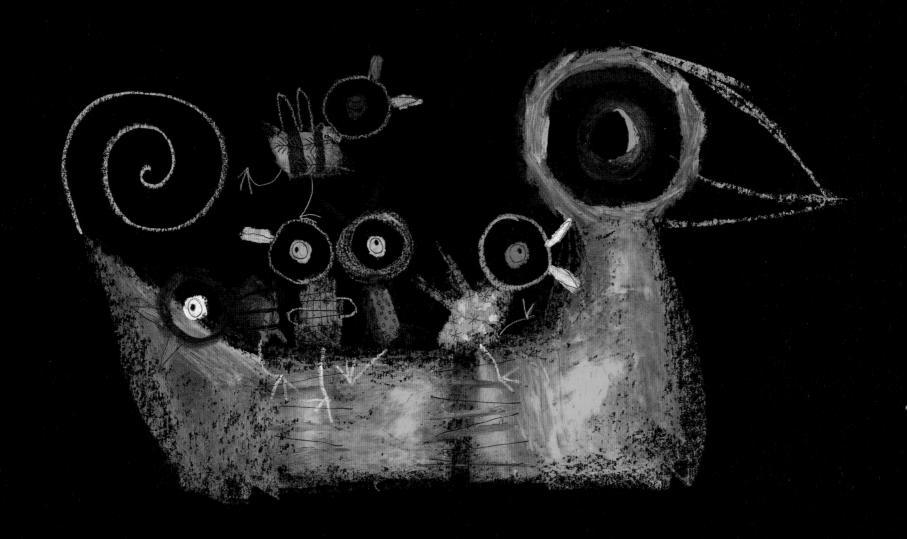

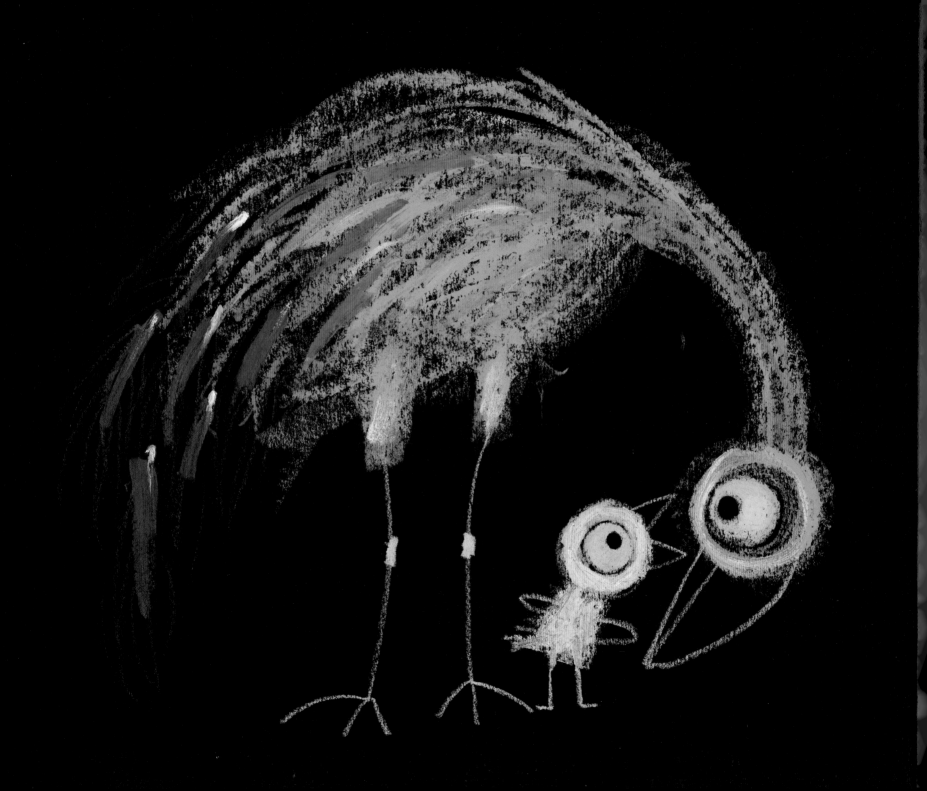

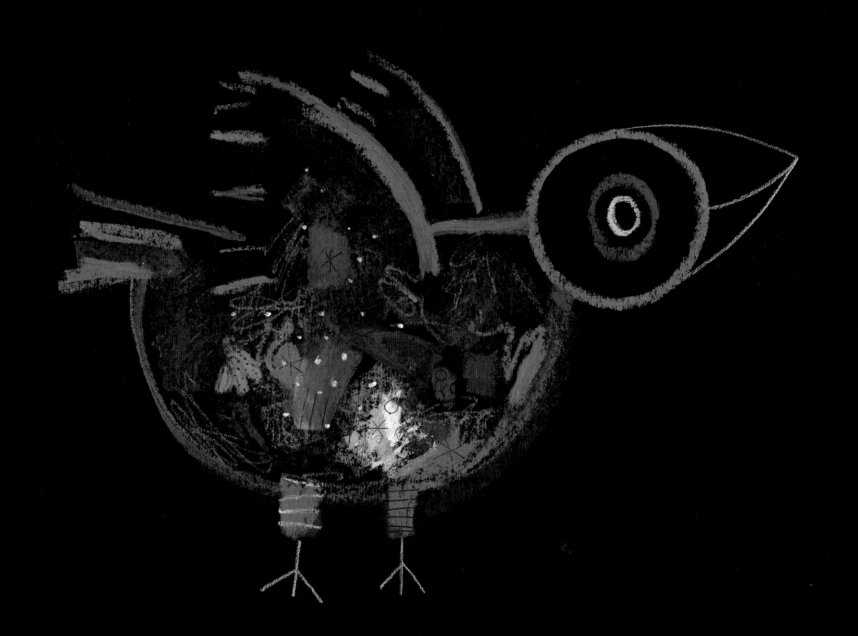

letting go

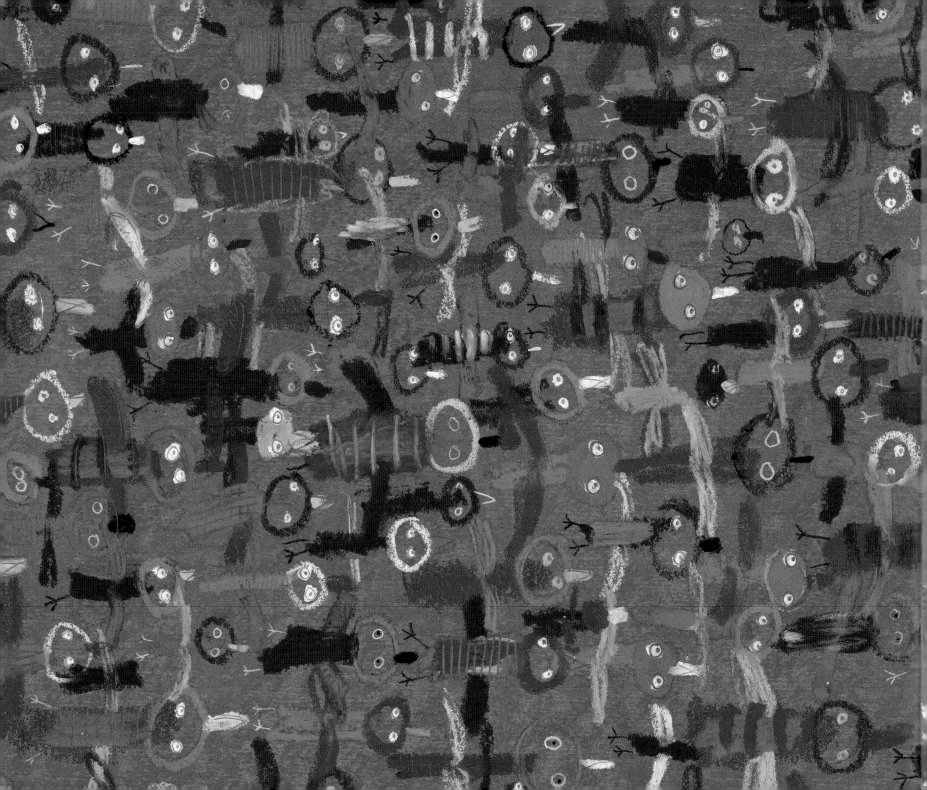